Filigree's Midnight Ride

AT THE HEELS OF HISTORY

HEELS OF HISTORY

Filigree's Midnight Ride

Pam Berkman and Dorothy Hearst
Illustrated by Claire Powell

Margaret K. McElderry Books

New York   London   Toronto   Sydney   New Delhi

MARGARET K. McELDERRY BOOKS

An imprint of Simon & Schuster Children's Publishing Division

1230 Avenue of the Americas, New York, New York 10020

This book is a work of fiction. Any references to historical events, real people, or real places are used fictitiously. Other names, characters, places, and events are products of the author's imagination, and any resemblance to actual events or places or persons, living or dead, is entirely coincidental.

MARGARET K. McELDERRY BOOKS is a trademark of Simon & Schuster, Inc.

For information about special discounts for bulk purchases, please contact Simon & Schuster Special Sales at 1-866-506-1949 or business@simonandschuster.com.

The Simon & Schuster Speakers Bureau can bring authors to your live event. For more information or to book an event, contact the Simon & Schuster Speakers Bureau at 1-866-248-3049 or visit our website at www.simonspeakers.com.

Also available in a Margaret K. McElderry Books paperback edition

Book design by Debra Sfetsios-Conover and Rebecca Syracuse

The text for this book was set in Caslon Old Face BT.

Cover art has been rendered by hand and colored in Photoshop.
All interior illustrations have been drawn by hand using pencil and graphite.

Manufactured in the United States of America

1019 FFG

First Margaret K. McElderry Books hardcover edition August 2019

2 4 6 8 10 9 7 5 3

CIP data for this book is available from the Library of Congress.

ISBN 978-1-5344-3332-8 (pbk)

ISBN 978-1-5344-3333-5 (hardcover)

ISBN 978-1-5344-3334-2 (eBook)

To Mehran, Brenna, Max,
Caspian, and Mom and Dad.
—P. B.

To my family, friends, and all the dogs.
And to Mom; you're here in every word I write.
—D. H.

Dedicated to my very own family historian,
Aunt Shirley. With love.
—C. P.

1
The Smallest Dog in Boston

April 18, 1775, Boston, Massachusetts

Filigree smelled danger and raced toward it. He flattened his ears against his head and stretched his short legs as far as he could. This was his chance. He leaped over a cobblestone as big as his head and dodged the wheels of a vegetable cart. He might be the smallest dog in

Boston, but he was ready to fight for freedom.

The street was wet and slippery with drizzle. Filigree dashed past a group of children throwing rotten eggs at British soldiers and laughing.

He rounded the corner onto Back Street. There he slid to a stop, panting. The fight had already begun.

It looked like every dog in Boston was

there. Jove, the huge Newfoundland, had cornered two British soldiers against a wall. Jove belonged to the patriot leader Samuel Adams. His head was as big as a pumpkin and his neck was as thick as a bull's. Dark shaggy fur covered his powerful chest.

His pack of patriot dogs surrounded him. Scout the spaniel stood with his front paws on the taller soldier's shoes. Rosie, a scruffy mutt, pulled on the smaller soldier's coat. All the other dogs yowled and snapped.

For the last ten years, many of the people of Boston had been angry about England controlling them. They called themselves patriots. But King George wouldn't even let them have a say about the laws they had to follow. Or the taxes they had to pay. Nearly two years ago, the patriots had thrown boxes and boxes of British tea into Boston Harbor because of the taxes on it. Patriots called that the Boston Tea Party.

After that, Jove decided the patriot dogs should stand up to the British too. They stole the soldiers' food, chased them when they were marching, and woke them up by howling in the middle of the night. Rosie once ran off with a whole leg of lamb meant for a general's dinner. Scout carried secret

messages tied to his collar.
Jove stood watch out-
side patriot meetings.

Filigree had been
ready to do his part, even
if he was only a five-pound Pomeranian. After
all, he belonged to nine-year-old Frances
Revere. She was the daughter of the patriot
Paul Revere. And Filigree was a patriot now
too. He had good reason to be.

"Reporting for duty, sir," he'd told Jove
the first time he'd seen him in North Square.
But Jove had laughed. "You're not even a real
dog. More like a dormouse," he'd said. "The

Redcoats won't even know you're there."

The patriots called the British soldiers "Redcoats" or "Lobsterbacks" because red was the human name for the color of their uniforms.

"A little pup like you could never make a difference," Jove had grunted.

His words had hit Filigree like a slap.

"Yes I can!" he'd barked. "And I'm not a pup!"

But Jove had just turned away. He'd started telling two sheepdogs how to pull tent pegs out of the ground to make the British army tents fall down.

Now, on Back Street, Rosie and Scout crouched low. They pulled their lips back to snarl at the soldiers.

Jove stepped forward and looked straight into the taller soldier's eyes. In dog language, that was a challenge to a fight. The fur on Filigree's back stood up.

The tall Redcoat raised the heavy wooden stock of his musket above Jove's head. He was going to dash Jove's brains out!

"No!" Filigree yapped. If anything happened to Jove, who would lead the patriot pack? The Redcoats weren't allowed to hurt children, but they had killed dogs.

The needle-sharp bayonet on the end of the Redcoat's gun caught the light of the setting sun. It glittered hard as silver ice.

Fear squeezed Filigree's chest. But he couldn't let the pack down. He charged toward Jove and the soldiers.

He took a running leap. He meant to land in front of the big dog and distract the Redcoat. But his jump didn't carry him quite as far as he wanted. He flew right into Jove's face.

Jove wasn't expecting a flying dog to hit him on the muzzle. He jumped back in surprise. The Redcoats saw their chance and ran.

The shorter one called over his shoulder, "General Gage will hang your masters when he catches them at their next Sons of Liberty meeting!" General Gage was the leader of the British troops in Boston.

"Wait until tonight!" the tall Lobsterback joined in. "They'll get what's coming to them!"

Rosie, Scout, and the other dogs pelted after them. Jove didn't follow. He was too

busy staring at Filigree in amazement.

The pack came panting back.

"They went inside a building," Rosie said. "We couldn't catch 'em."

"But we sure showed those Lobsterbacks whose street this is!" Filigree barked.

Jove was still staring at him. Filigree stood as tall as he could. His nose was lined up with Jove's knee. He wagged his tail in triumph. He had saved Jove! He waited for the big dog to thank him.

Jove growled and showed his sharp, sharp teeth. "Fool!" he barked. "You ruined everything!"

2

A Useless Dormouse

"Useless dormouse!" Rosie rumbled.

"Lapdog," Scout growled. He sat down in disgust.

Fool! Lapdog! The words stung Filigree's ears. "That Redcoat was going to pound your head in!" he yipped at Jove.

"I knew exactly where his musket was!"

Jove thundered. "And I knew how to dodge it! As soon as he tried to hit me, I would've knocked him over on his backside. He wouldn't have been able to march for a month!" He gave a huff. "True patriots do what they can, when they can! You wouldn't understand. Everyone knows you used to belong to a loyalist!"

Filigree flinched. It was true. He used to live with Mrs. Amelia Banks. She was married to a wealthy merchant. Like many rich colonists, she was loyal to King George in England. She had always been good to Filigree. He had slept on a silk pillow right next to her.

And he had lost her because of the Redcoats and King George.

Filigree's spine stiffened and so did his tail. He wouldn't let *anyone* say he wasn't a patriot.

"I'm just as much a patriot as you are, Jove Adams!" he barked. "Mr. Revere is a Son of Liberty just like Mr. Adams! He's the best spy in Boston. And—"

Jove's large paw came down on top of him.

"My whole plan ruined by a little runt

who could fit into a sugar bowl!" Jove muttered. "Stay home and leave the fighting to the real dogs and the real patriots."

Filigree wanted to tell Jove he *was* a real dog, but he couldn't breathe under Jove's paw. If he could get a breath in, he would also tell Jove that he knew nothing was more important than freedom.

The day Filigree became a patriot was the hardest day of his life.

The British had wanted to punish the patriots for the Boston Tea Party. They closed

Boston Harbor. They said that the people who governed the colony of Massachusetts Bay had to be appointed by them. British soldiers barged into colonists' homes whenever they wanted. And the people of Boston could only have town meetings once a year.

Mrs. Banks hadn't liked that. "I don't see what's wrong with people meeting together, Pudding," she had said. "Pudding" was Filigree's name back then.

So Mrs. Banks had let some patriots visit her house. "I'm sure King George didn't mean they can't talk in my sitting room," she told Filigree.

But it turned out that was exactly what King George meant.

The Redcoats stormed the house. The patriots barely got out in time. Mr. Banks was so angry, he said Mrs. Banks had to go back to England to live with his sister.

The very next morning he put her in a carriage that would take her to a ship at Plymouth Harbor.

"You're not taking that ball of fluff with you!" Mr. Banks said when he saw Filigree. "My sister hates dogs."

He wrenched Filigree away from Mrs.

Banks and dumped him on the ground.

Mrs. Banks shouted. Filigree barked. He leaped with all of his might, but he couldn't jump back into the carriage. "Wait!" Filigree cried. But the carriage rattled out of sight.

"All she did was let people talk in her house!" Filigree howled. He howled and howled until his voice was gone. *It's not right for one group of people to tell another group what to do like that!* he thought.

He lay down in the middle of the street with his head on his paws. He didn't care what happened to him anymore.

The sun was high when a pair of boots stopped in front of him.

"Why, it's Mrs. Banks's dog," said a rich voice. It was Mr. Revere, one of the patriots who had been at Mrs. Banks's house.

"My little girl Frances is sick," he said. "She's had rheumatic fever. I think you just might cheer her up." He put Filigree into his big coat pocket.

It didn't matter to Filigree. He whimpered all the way to the Revere home at 19 North Square and up the stairs to the room Frances shared with two of her sisters. He didn't realize his fluffy white tail stuck out of Mr. Revere's pocket like a feather.

"Papa!" he heard a hoarse voice cry. "Did you bring me a bird?"

"No, Frances," Mr. Revere answered. "Not a bird." He drew Filigree out of his pocket. Filigree saw a girl sitting up in bed. Her face was pale and she was thinner than the other children he had met.

Her dark eyes sparkled. "He's perfect!"

Filigree couldn't help himself. He wagged his tail, just a bit.

Mr. Revere sat on the bed.

"This little dog has just lost someone he loved," Mr. Revere said. "He's going to be sad for a while. I want you two to watch over each other. You're still not strong, Frances."

"I am too." Frances pulled Filigree into her arms.

Mr. Revere whispered in Filigree's ear, "Take care of my girl. I'm trusting you now, boy. Don't let me down."

No one had ever asked Filigree to take care of anyone before.

And Mrs. Banks would want him to help a little girl, wouldn't she? Filigree licked Frances's cheek.

I'll take care of her, he snuffled even though he knew Mr. Revere couldn't understand him.

And he would make sure the British could never take anyone away from him—or anyone else—ever again.

But all Jove and the pack cared about was that Mrs. Banks had once been loyal to King George.

Jove stepped off Filigree. He looked over his pack. "Time to get to work, patriots!" he barked.

"Should I head to the British camp?" asked Scout. "Find out what they're up to?"

Jove woofed a *yes*. "Rosie," he ordered, "I saw some barrels being carried into the mess tent. Must be ale for the soldiers to drink. Push over as many as you can and see if you can knock some holes into them."

"What about me?" Filigree wheezed. He was still getting his breath back from being under Jove. But he wasn't going to give up. Ever. "I can . . . I can . . ."

"There's nothing you can do," muttered
Jove.

Rosie sighed. "Just stay out of our way,
Dormouse."

Filigree had never felt so small.

"What about you, sir?" piped up Scout.

"I have other duties," Jove answered. His chest swelled. "Mr. Adams is in Lexington with Mr. Hancock. Got to get a ride there across Boston Neck. Patriot business tonight."

He and the pack trotted away.

Filigree stood alone on Back Street. The sun was almost down.

He'd had his chance. He'd failed. He'd never be part of the patriot pack.

3
The Revere House

The last rays of the April sun didn't warm Filigree. When a squadron of Redcoats marched down the street toward their camp on Boston Common, he didn't even bother to growl at them.

Behind them, the pack of dogs who were loyal to the British marched in formation.

They had been Filigree's friends once. He pretended not to see them. But he couldn't help hearing them.

"Traitor," muttered their leader, Queenie, as she passed him. She was a strong, solid fox-hound. Then she barked, "L-e-e-eft turn!" The pack headed around the corner toward Boston Common and the British camp.

Filigree's tail drooped as he returned to the Revere home. There was a tiny hole cut in the door just for him. He wriggled through it.

There were good smells coming from the kitchen in the cellar. Filigree's mouth watered.

Jove's insults still hurt, but he was hungry. He followed the smells down the stairs.

Frances's older sisters, Deborah and Sarah, were cooking pork and hasty pudding for dinner. The meat sizzled and spat on the stove. Sarah tossed Filigree a piece. He leaped and caught it. The fatty, salty flavor cheered him up a little.

Then he spotted the Reveres' house cat,

Anvil. She curled on the kitchen floor like a round black rug. She was between Filigree and his water bowl.

"Trouble with the patriot pack again?" she mewed.

"No," Filigree said. "I saved Jove."

"That's not what I heard." Anvil *always* seemed to find out about things.

"At least *I* try to help," Filigree growled. "You just lie there."

Anvil yawned and stretched so she took up more of the floor.

Filigree walked the long way around her to his bowl. He lapped up his water. "I *did*

save Jove's life," he mumbled. "He couldn't have dodged that gun."

He padded up the stairs and into the big front room to find Frances.

He couldn't see where she was, but he could smell her. She smelled like vanilla and herbs. Her father was sitting with Dr. Warren at a table in the corner. Dr. Warren was Frances's doctor, but Filigree knew he was also one of the patriot leaders. The two men bent over a piece of paper and whispered. Filigree heard the words "ride" and "lanterns" and "patrols," and something about General Gage.

Paul Revere looked up at Filigree. "She's upstairs in her room, boy," he said.

No, she's not, Filigree thought.

There was a big armchair near the winding staircase. Filigree trotted over and crawled under it. Frances was sitting cross-legged behind the chair. It was her favorite spy-on-the-family place. She was mushed up against the wall. Her dark eyes were fierce. *What's wrong?* Filigree wondered.

When no one was looking, Frances picked

up Filigree and tiptoed upstairs with him in her arms. He could feel her heart beating fast against him.

None of her sisters was in the bedroom. Frances plunked down on the edge of her bed. Filigree settled into her lap.

Anvil jumped up beside them.

"I was here first!" Filigree barked.

"*I* was in this house when you were still eating crumpets and tea cakes with the loyalists," Anvil hissed.

Filigree would have answered back, but he could tell Frances was upset.

"I heard them talking," Frances said.

"General Gage won't put up with the patriots anymore. He's going to send the Redcoats to Lexington to arrest Mr. Adams and Mr. Hancock." *What?!* Filigree stood up in her lap. "Dr. Warren just doesn't know when," Frances went on. "He told Papa to be ready to ride to warn them when the time comes. Deborah says General Gage will hang Mr.

Adams and Mr. Hancock if he catches them.
But what if he catches Papa instead and hangs
him?"

Anvil crowded into Frances's lap. Filigree
shoved the cat with his shoulder. It didn't do
any good.

"If Mr. Revere knows what's good for
him," Anvil meowed, "he'll stay home."

"They wouldn't really hang him, would
they?" Filigree asked. He hated to ask Anvil
anything, but he needed to know.

"No one is supposed to help the patriots,"
Anvil said. "And nobody's allowed out after
dark."

Filigree knew about that. It was called a "curfew." It meant that anyone out at night could be arrested.

Frances stood up, tumbling Filigree and Anvil onto the bed. "I won't just sit around and wait!" She paced back and forth between the beds.

The family still treated Frances like she was sick. Mr. Revere said she had to have her supper in bed and stay in the house almost all the time. Only Filigree knew that Frances sneaked out to run and play catch with him and was getting stronger every day.

Frances sat down on the bed, crossed her

arms, and lay down with a thump. "I'm not going to lose Papa, too," she said. It had been less than two years since her mother died. Filigree knew that Frances still missed her every day.

Anvil jumped off the bed and stalked away.

"Where are you going?" Filigree demanded. "We have to figure out what to do."

"I'm going to catch mice," Anvil answered. "That's *my* job."

"Useless cat rug," Filigree said. He climbed onto Frances's pillow and curled up beside her.

Filigree opened his eyes. He didn't know when he had fallen asleep. Moonlight streamed in through the window. Frances and her sisters were all sleeping. It must be very late.

He realized what had woken him. He could hear the firm tread of Mr. Revere downstairs. He nudged Frances.

"What is it, Filigree?" Frances murmured sleepily. Then, "Yes. Yes, I hear Papa."

Then came the sound of voices and of a door opening and closing.

"Why is Papa going out after dark?" Frances whispered.

Especially tonight, Filigree thought. Jove had said something important was happening. So had the Redcoats.

Frances and Filigree looked at each other.

Something's wrong.

4

Into the Boston Night

They padded silently through Mr. and Mrs. Revere's bedroom. It was empty. Filigree made sure his toenails didn't click on the wooden floor. At the stairway, his ears and nose twitched, alert. He stayed on guard all the way downstairs. Frances's stepmother sat at the table in the main room, holding Mr. Revere's leather bag.

Frances darted behind the armchair. Filigree followed. He tried to breathe quietly. They waited for what seemed like a long time.

Finally the door opened. Mr. Revere was back. He strode into the room and walked over to Frances's stepmother.

"It's happening, Rachel," he said. He didn't sit down. "Warren says the Regulars are heading to Concord tonight to take our supplies." "Regulars" was another name for Redcoats. "And they're on their way to arrest Adams and Hancock. I'm going across the river and riding to Lexington to warn them. William Dawes is already on his way there. If one of us is caught, maybe the other will get through."

Filigree felt Frances tense beside him. He pressed up against her. "And the signal . . . ?" Frances's stepmother began.

Mr. Revere's voice was grim. "Our friend

Newman is on his way to the Old North Church to hang the lanterns. That will let our men know the Regulars are coming across the river. Our men will ride out to the towns and farms to warn everyone they can." He put his arm around his wife's shoulders. "Rachel . . . if I'm caught . . ."

"The Redcoats will be happy to hang the spy Paul Revere," she finished. "So you'd best keep ahead of them." She slung his leather bag over his shoulder.

Mr. Revere walked out into the night.

"Stay alive," Frances's stepmother whispered to the closed door. She shut the latch.

Filigree saw her feet go by as she walked upstairs.

As soon as she was gone, Filigree sprang onto the armchair. Frances stood up. She was trembling. "Hang the spy Paul Revere! Oh, Filigree!" She bent down to bury her nose in his fur. He woofed in sympathy.

"I'm going after him!" Frances whispered. "I can warn him if anyone follows him. I'm so small, those Lobsterbacks won't even see me."

Me either, Filigree thought. He jumped down from the chair.

"Are you coming with me?" Frances asked.

Of course I am. Filigree was already

running toward the door. The patriots would need all the help they could get.

Frances put on her shoes.

Filigree felt a twinge.

Take care of my girl, Mr. Revere had said that day he brought Filigree home. *I'm trusting you.*

Maybe she shouldn't go.

But to protect Frances, Filigree had to protect the patriots. Especially her father. Besides, he knew that Frances would go no matter what. If she went, he was going with her.

Frances reached up and unlatched the door so slowly, it didn't make any noise. She opened the door a crack. Filigree nudged it farther so they could both slip through. They stepped outside together.

They had only taken a few steps when a booming voice stopped them.

"What are you doing here?" it demanded.

Filigree's left front paw froze in midair.

He looked way, way up. Right into the face of General Gage, leader of the Redcoat army.

5
General Gage

The general towered over them. His jaw looked as set and still as stone. Filigree felt miles and miles below him, as if General Gage were a tree or a mountain sticking up through the clouds.

Filigree shook like the mouse that Anvil had cornered by the stove that morning.

They were caught.

Then the general spoke.

"Why, if it isn't Pudding!" he exclaimed.
He put his hands on his knees. "Mrs.
Banks's little Pomeranian!" He patted
Filigree's head. "I didn't realize she'd left
you in Boston. What are you doing out at
this hour? Are you lost?"

He's only talking to me! Filigree realized.
He doesn't see Frances!

Filigree could just hear Frances breathing fast behind him. She must be curled in the deep frame of the low window peeking into the Revere's cellar. That was another of her favorite spying places. She was hidden—for now.

His next thought was, *Please don't let anyone in the patriot pack hear General Gage call me Pudding.*

They would never stop laughing at him. And that was nothing compared to what they would do if they found out that he knew General Gage! The general used to come to tea with Mrs. Banks. She called him "Thomas My Lad" and his American wife

"Peggy Dear." Filigree always found it hard to believe that Thomas My Lad was the same person as the fearsome General Gage.

He had to make sure the general didn't look Frances's way. If General Gage saw a little girl out at night, he would start knocking on doors, including the one at 19 North Square. He would find out that Mr. Revere wasn't home in bed like he should have been.

Filigree jumped up and licked the general's nose. Then he ran in a circle and yipped. That was how they used to play together. "That's my Pudding!" the general laughed.

Suddenly the smell of gunpowder and damp wool wafted under Filigree's nose. It got closer and closer. There was no mistaking that smell—the scent of a Redcoat uniform. Then he heard the quick clomp-clomp of a soldier walking briskly up to them. General Gage stood up straight as a musket and stopped laughing.

"General," the soldier said. "I'm sorry to tell you, sir. We have word that the rebels know about our plans. Some of them might try to cross the Charles River tonight to warn their militia that we're coming."

The general's voice reminded Filigree of Jove when he growled. "I want more patrols at the river, Captain," he said. "Order them to arrest anyone at the river's edge or anyone who tries to cross it. If they have to shoot those rebel villains, shoot them."

"Yes, sir," said the captain. As he turned, his buttons flashed in the moonlight. He clomped away even faster than he had come.

"I'm sorry, Pudding," General Gage said. "I can't play tonight."

He took a piece of shortbread out of his pocket and tossed it to Filigree. Filigree gulped it down. He knew General Gage was the enemy, but he hadn't had dinner. And shortbread was shortbread.

The general stomped off.

Small hands grabbed Filigree. Frances had come up behind him. She pulled him close.

"We have to get to the river before Papa does," she said. "We have to warn him the Redcoats know what he's doing!" She set Filigree down and ran.

Above Filigree, a low meow sounded. He looked up at the windowsill. Anvil's unblinking amber eyes gazed down at him. She had a dead mouse in her mouth. Its tail hung down like a string. She crunched and swallowed.

"Was that Redcoat shortbread tasty?" she mewed. "Not much of a patriot, are you?

Pudding." Then she leaped out of sight.

"More than you are," Filigree muttered.

Frances was already far ahead of him. Filigree took off after her. He caught up with her at the corner of Charter Street and Henchman Lane.

"I'm going to be Papa's eyes and ears, Filigree," Frances whispered. "I'm going to ride with him."

Filigree wasn't at all sure that Mr. Revere would let her do that. Either way, he would stay by her side.

They hurried up Lynn Street toward the river. Frances moved so quickly, Filigree had to run to keep up.

The paving stones were still slick from the rain earlier that day. Colorless mists swirled like ghosts out of doorways and alleys.

They had just passed the entrance to Baker's Shipyard near the water when Filigree heard paws padding on packed dirt.

He smelled dogs in the shipyard. But there was no Rosie or Scout or even Jove.

These dogs were the enemy. The pack loyal to the British. And they were on his trail.

6
The Loyalist Pack

Filigree let Frances run on ahead. He turned back toward the shipyard and the loyalist dogs.

He couldn't let them follow Frances. If they did, they'd find Mr. Revere. They'd start up a yapping that could wake King George himself across the ocean. Redcoats would come running.

He dashed into the shipyard and waited. He could see a half-built ship, a schooner, looming up on a frame. It looked like a giant's wooden skeleton. A foxhound stepped from the shadows beneath it.

"Hello, Queenie," Filigree said.

The leader of the loyalist dogs stood very still. Her tail curved high above her. "Why, look who's here," she said. "If it isn't that little turncoat, Pudding." She didn't snarl, like Jove might have. She sounded cool and calm. Which was much worse.

Her pack marched out of the darkness at the edges of the shipyard. They formed two straight lines behind Queenie. Filigree recognized a tall poodle named Chaucer, and Biscuit and Gravy, twin terriers. Half a dozen other dogs—setters, mastiffs, collies—stood with them. They were all perfectly washed and combed and trimmed. But they were tough. And they were all bigger than Filigree.

"Forward!" ordered Queenie. The pack stalked toward Filigree in formation. They crossed the big square of ground where the boats were built. They surrounded him beneath the moonlight.

"He's not Pudding anymore," Biscuit said. "He has a new name now."

"What is it?" Gravy laughed. "Custard?"

Filigree growled. He loved his name. Frances had given it to him.

"It's Filigree," Queenie said. "Because he belongs to that traitor silversmith. The spy Paul Revere. You know what we do to traitors and spies, don't you, Filigree?"

The entire pack lowered their heads and growled.

"We dump them in the river," Chaucer woofed.

Filigree couldn't let them get to the river and see Mr. Revere!

What would Jove do? He would stop them!

Earlier, in the fight with the Redcoats, Filigree's aim had been off. This time, he'd do better.

"You just try it!" he woofed.

He hurled himself at Queenie as hard as he could.

It felt like hitting a brick wall. He fell. Before he could get back up, Biscuit shoved him with his muzzle. Filigree rolled over twice. He jumped on Biscuit's back. Gravy knocked him off.

"Take the little traitor prisoner!" barked Queenie. "To the river!" The loyalist pack closed in on Filigree. A big collie picked him up by

the scruff of his neck. Filigree struggled as hard as he could. It did no good.

Then Filigree heard loud barking

and paws running up the street. Rosie, Scout, and the other patriot dogs raced into the shipyard. They jumped on the loyalists.

"We heard Queenie!" Scout growled.

"We *told* you to stay out of our way!" Rosie barked. She butted at the collie until he dropped Filigree. "We have better things to do tonight than rescue you!"

"I don't need rescuing!" Filigree barked, even though it wasn't true.

He watched Rosie chase Chaucer back under the skeleton ship. Scout and a large hound struggled with Queenie. Filigree scrambled toward them.

"Get out of here!" cried Scout. "You can't do any good!" Filigree wanted to sink into the ground.

"I'm staying to fight!" he woofed.

But he couldn't. Frances needed him to help her watch over Mr. Revere. He had to go to her, no matter what the patriot pack thought of him.

It was one of the hardest things he had ever done, but Filigree ran from the shipyard. The sounds of the fight got farther away. He saw a small dark shape moving down Lynn Street toward him. Frances was coming back for him. He ran to meet her.

"There you are!" Frances panted. "I saw Papa go down Freeman's wharf!"

All along the river, wharves stuck out into the water. Filigree and Frances raced toward one of them. At the end of it, Mr. Revere moved like a dark ghost. As they watched, he jumped down under the wharf.

"He must have a boat hidden!" Frances whispered.

Filigree's nose twitched.

Gunpowder. Damp wool.

Three Redcoats rounded the corner and marched down the wharf—right toward Mr. Revere.

7
Freeman's Wharf

Filigree's tail shot straight up. Frances froze. They stumbled into the shadows of the barrels and crates that lined the wharf.

"They'll see Papa," Frances gasped. She knelt and looked into Filigree's eyes.

"Listen, Filigree," she said firmly. "The Lobsterbacks will see me if I go to Papa, and then they'll see him, too. But they won't notice *you*. I'm going to distract them. I can't be his eyes and ears now. You have to be. Stay here until I get rid of the soldiers. Then go on with Papa without me."

No! Filigree thought. He couldn't let her do that! He was supposed to take care of her—forever! That was why he'd made such a fool of himself in the shipyard. He couldn't fail at this, too!

Frances stood. She walked away from him. Filigree scampered after her.

Frances turned. "Stay," she mouthed. *Oh, Frances!* Filigree thought. But he stayed. He still tensed his back legs, ready to get to her if she needed him.

She ran out in front of the soldiers. All three men stopped short and looked down at her.

"In heaven's name, what are you doing out here??" one of them said. "Little girl, it's dangerous to be out tonight."

"Where are your parents?" said the second one. "Where do you live?"

"On Essex Street," Frances lied.

"That's all the way on the other side of Boston!" the first Redcoat said.

"I want to go home," Frances said. "But, um . . . I saw . . ."

Filigree could tell she was trying to think of something. He panted with worry. What if the Redcoats figured out she was tricking them?

"A bear!" Frances said at last. "I saw a bear on Foster Lane!"

The soldiers laughed. The third one, who looked as big as a bear himself, said, "I don't think there are any bears in Boston, little girl."

"Yes, yes, there is. I saw it!" Frances said.

The soldier snickered. "Still, we can't have you wandering around alone at night," he said. "Especially tonight."

"I'd rather take her home than stay here and deal with the Yankee rebels," said one of the others. He popped a walnut into his mouth. "And we're supposed to keep the Boston children safe."

They began to lead Frances away. Filigree couldn't stand it. He couldn't leave her in the hands of Redcoats.

He took a step toward her.

A large ball of fur plopped down in front of him from the roof of a shed.

It was Anvil.

"What do you think you're doing?" she spat. "Frances told you to go!"

Filigree couldn't believe his eyes. "What are you doing here?"

"You think you're the only patriot in the house? I've been keeping an eye on the two of you all the way from North Square. I'll get her home. You know her; she'll slip away from them. She knows every doorway and alley in Boston. And the Lobsterbacks aren't allowed to hurt children. You have to make sure Mr. Revere gets to Lexington."

"I thought your job was catching mice! Why do you suddenly care about the patriots?" Filigree demanded.

Anvil hissed, "I've been a patriot since you were a pup. We just didn't know if we could trust you. You lived with that loyalist for years. We're still not sure about you. But we don't have a choice."

"Who's *we*?" Filigree asked. He looked up. At least a dozen cats of all shapes and sizes were hiding in the shadows. They crouched on top of barrels and peered out of crates.

"We're ready when you are, General," one of them meowed to Anvil.

"General?" Filigree repeated. "You're a *general*?"

Then he shook himself.

"I won't leave Frances!" he insisted.

Anvil swatted him across the nose. "Mr. Revere needs you now! Are you a patriot or not? Or do you only want to help when it's easy?"

Filigree looked toward Frances. She was

turning a corner with the soldiers.

GO! she mouthed over her shoulder. *Please!*

"Go," said Anvil. "I'll watch over her."

Anvil slunk away to follow the Redcoats and Frances. One by one, the other cats stalked after him.

Filigree looked at Frances one last time. Then he made his decision.

He ran down to the very end of the wharf.

He jumped from the wooden planks onto the sand below. Mr. Revere and two other men were tugging and pulling at something. It was a rowboat.

"Softly as you can, Thomas," Mr. Revere

whispered. "Joshua, take care of the oars."

Joshua nodded. He tied lengths of cloth around the iron oarlocks. It made them quieter. He looked up and saw Filigree.

"Revere," he said, "we have a visitor. Isn't that your dog?"

Mr. Revere turned.

"Good heavens! What are you doing out here, Filigree?" His face was stern. "Go home, boy."

Filigree stayed where he was.

"Bad dog. Home!" Mr. Revere pointed toward North Square.

Filigree thought his heart would rip in

two. No one had ever called him a bad dog. Not once.

"Now!" Mr. Revere said, still pointing. He stared until Filigree started to walk away. Then Mr. Revere turned back to the boat.

Filigree wanted more than anything to be a good dog. But Mr. Revere needed him, even if he didn't know it. Filigree stopped walking and looked back at the river.

He had always gone home when he was told to. Mr. Revere wouldn't think he would disobey now.

The men slipped the boat into the water. Mr. Revere got in while the other two held it.

No one was looking at Filigree. They were all busy launching the boat.

True patriots do what they can, when they can.

Filigree ran toward the boat. His paws made no sound in the soft sand. He jumped with all his strength.

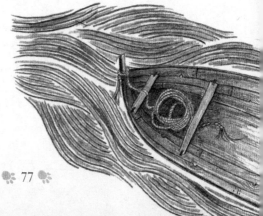

8
The HMS Somerset

Filigree dove under the wooden platform at the back of the boat. He found himself standing in very cold water. It came all the way up to his chest. Mr. Revere and the two other men sat on wooden plank benches in front of him. The moon was low in the sky. It shone bright on the river.

The boat rocked and the water sloshed. The men rowed away from the wharf.

Filigree dug his toes into the bottom of the boat to keep from falling. He almost fell anyway, because suddenly he was startled by a noise.

It was the growl of a huge animal, and it was right above him.

He tensed his legs, ready to fight if the animal attacked.

But something was strange. He couldn't *smell* any animal.

Carefully, he put his front paws up on the bench behind Thomas to look over one side of the rowboat.

This was no animal. It was the British warship, the HMS *Somerset*, looming like a great crouching beast above them. It was taller than two houses and as long as ten rowboats. It creaked with a sound like a lion's roar.

They would have to pass right under the huge ship.

Filigree saw that all the rowboats, canoes, and rafts that usually floated on the river had been tied to the *Somerset*'s side. The Redcoats must have taken them all, to try to keep anyone from crossing tonight. They would be looking for patriots on the river.

People moved around like giant ants on the ship's deck. Filigree made sure to stay low, behind Thomas's broad back.

"Revere, they'll be on the watch for us," Thomas hissed.

"Steady, boys," whispered Mr. Revere. "No talking until we're past the ship."

Mr. Revere's jaw was clenched. The muscles on Thomas's back were tense. But the men stayed calm. They rowed steadily across the river. Filigree tried to stay calm too. A patriot had to face danger.

They came right up next to the *Somerset*. Their little boat was so close to the side of the ship, the men could almost have touched it. Filigree could smell men, tar, and the gunpowder of the ship's big cannons.

Then, on the ship, he saw a line of sailors looking out over the river. His legs shook. All the sailors had to do was look down and they would see the rowboat. The night was so bright with moonlight, there was nowhere to hide. They were going to be seen!

All at once they were in darkness. *What happened?* Filigree peered out from behind Thomas's back. The moon was so low, it cast a black shadow from behind the *Somerset* onto the water. The rowboat slid into the shadow.

It was so dark there, the sailors couldn't see them! Filigree held his breath. The patriots glided on silently, out of sight of the British warship. Filigree exhaled. He wanted to tell the moon, "Thank you."

Suddenly the ship's bell rang out, five great clangs. Filigree jumped and so did Thomas, Joshua, and Mr. Revere. Filigree dove back under the bench. Then all was quiet on the water.

"Five bells," grunted Joshua, using all his strength to row.

"That'd make it about ten thirty," whispered Thomas.

"Quiet," shushed Mr. Revere. "Not much longer now."

Filigree peeked out again.

Before them, coming up fast, was the shore and Charlestown Battery.

The Battery was made up of wharves and docks, smaller than the ones in Boston. The boat bumped to a stop. Mr. Revere, Thomas, and Joshua stepped out. They tied the boat to the dock with a long rope.

Filigree climbed up onto the bench so that he could jump to shore. But the shore was too far away.

Mr. Revere was going to leave without him!

9
Brown Beauty

He couldn't come all this way and be left behind!

He jumped into the river.

Water ran up his nose and into his ears. His bottom half sunk under the water. He drifted away from the riverbank. The current of the river turned him around. His heart sped up. What if he floated all the way out to sea?!

He paddled as hard as he could. Somehow, he turned himself in the right direction and made it to the bank.

He climbed out, dripping and shivering.

Mr. Revere and his friends were talking to some other men.

"The Regulars are coming over the river," Mr. Revere said.

"Yes. We saw the lanterns," another man said. Filigree recognized the voice of Mr. Revere's friend Mr. Devens. "The other riders have left. They'll stop in towns along the way to send out more men. They'll all ride to Concord."

To stop the Redcoats from seizing the patriots' supplies! Filigree remembered.

Mr. Revere nodded. "But my mission is in Lexington. I need to warn Adams and Hancock. They're meeting at Reverend Clarke's house. Have you got a fast horse for me?"

"The fastest horse in Massachusetts," Mr. Devens said. "John Larkin's mare, Brown Beauty. She's saddled and ready." Everyone knew Brown Beauty.

Filigree ran into town as fast as he could.

He crept into the dark stable and into Brown Beauty's stall.

"Patriot business," he woofed softly. Brown Beauty looked down. She let out a loud, snuffly snort.

"Don't bother me, dog," she neighed.

"You're taking Mr. Revere to Lexington, and I need to come along," Filigree said as firmly as he could.

Brown Beauty lowered her big head. "You?

That's a joke." She picked up some hay in her big teeth and began to chomp.

"It's no joke!" Filigree woofed. "We have to warn Mr. Adams and Mr. Hancock that the Lobsterbacks are coming to arrest them!"

Brown Beauty stopped chomping. She swallowed her mouthful of hay. "That's tonight?" she whinnied. "I'm ready." She stomped a hoof.

"Good," Filigree said. "Let me up."

"You'd just be in the way," Brown Beauty said.

"I'm coming with you," Filigree said. "Mr. Revere needs me." He jumped as high as he could. He couldn't get anywhere near the saddle. He tried again.

Brown Beauty flicked her tail at him as if he were a fly. "Not a chance," she said.

Filigree thought hard.

He turned and began to walk away. "I understand," he said over his shoulder. "If I'm too heavy for you . . . I wouldn't want to slow you down."

Brown Beauty lifted her head and shook her mane. "Don't be ridiculous. I once raced a ship from the bay to the sea and I won. You think you can slow *me* down? We'll see about that! Get on."

Filigree ran up a slanted piece of wood onto the narrow ledge of the stall door. There he stopped. It was a long, long way to Brown Beauty's back. *Maybe this is a bad idea*, he thought.

"Are you coming or not?" she snorted. "I have patriots to save."

"I'm coming." Filigree jumped. He landed on Brown Beauty's saddle. It was slippery. He almost fell. He slid down

the saddle and squirmed into the saddlebag.
The flap fell down over his head.

The door to the stable opened. Mr. Devens
came in and led Brown Beauty from the stall.
Outside, Mr. Revere waited. He leaped up
onto the horse's back. Filigree felt him kick
her side. Brown Beauty reared up on her back
legs.

"To Lexington!" she neighed.

10
The Midnight Ride

*Filigree slid down to the bottom of the saddle-*bag. Brown Beauty landed on all four hooves and began to trot.

He stuck his nose out from under the flap. He felt Brown Beauty go from the jolt-jolt-jolt of trotting to the smooth flow of a gallop. She ran faster than Filigree had ever moved before.

The scents of the town flew back and forth under Filigree's nose. River water. Pigs. Chickens. Smoke from dying hearth fires.

Mr. Revere turned Brown Beauty onto Charlestown Common. Filigree smelled marsh grass and mud.

Then he sniffed it. Gunpowder and wool.

Redcoats. Mr. Revere was riding straight toward them.

"Brown Beauty!" Filigree woofed softly. "Stop!"

She didn't hear him. Her hooves kept pounding against the dirt. Filigree threw himself against the saddlebag, trying to make it slam against Brown Beauty's side. Nothing happened.

He pushed his head out of the saddle-bag, then wriggled his front paws and chest through. Just then, Brown Beauty leaped over a fallen branch and Filigree almost bounced out. He held on for his life.

They were getting closer to the Redcoats. There was only one thing to do.

"Stop! Stop! Stop!" he barked.

Brown Beauty flicked back her ears. Mr. Revere looked down. He saw Filigree.

"What the . . . ?" he spluttered.

He pulled up on Brown Beauty's reins and she stopped.

"Oh no," he said. "Oh no, oh no, oh no. How did you get here? I TOLD YOU TO GO HOME." Mr. Revere was whispering, but he was so angry, it was worse than shouting. He shook his finger at Filigree, and Filigree wanted to cry. His tail fell between his legs, and his ears went flat against his head.

But he couldn't take the time to cry now. He strained in the direction the scent was coming from. It was up ahead, under a cluster of trees.

He whimpered a tiny whimper, trying to be as quiet as he could. Frantically he pointed with his nose. A dark shadow moved, just a little, under one of the birch trees. There were two Redcoats sitting on horseback, hiding under the branches.

Mr. Revere saw. His eyes widened.

He turned and galloped.

The Redcoats had seen him. They kicked their horses into a gallop. One was coming straight for Brown Beauty. The other raced ahead onto the road. He was trying to head off Mr. Revere!

But Mr. Revere was the best rider in Boston, and Brown Beauty was the fastest horse in Massachusetts. Mr. Revere cut across the road toward a hedge. Brown Beauty jumped it. The Redcoat's horse tried to follow, but he wouldn't jump the hedge. The soldier ahead on the road tried to catch up, but Brown Beauty was too fast for him. The soldier gave up the chase and turned back.

"Scruffy Yankee rebel!" his horse shouted at Brown Beauty.

"You just wish you were as fast as she is!" Filigree woofed back.

Brown Beauty whinnied a laugh. "No snobby Redcoat could *ever* catch me!" she taunted. She sped up. Filigree felt the wind stream past his ears. He knew they were in danger. But he couldn't help enjoying himself.

When they had gotten farther away from the soldiers, Mr. Revere slowed Brown Beauty to a walk. He whistled low through his teeth. "I never would have seen them in time. I would have ridden straight into them." He looked down at Filigree. Filigree peeked anxiously out of the saddlebag. Was Mr. Revere still angry with him?

"You sensed them before I did, didn't you? Or smelled them? Good dog," he murmured. He scooped Filigree out of the saddlebag. He put him into his own leather bag, the one he wore across his chest. "You let me know right away, now," he said, "if you smell any more of them."

Filigree's tail thumped against Mr. Revere's chest.

They galloped on. But soon Mr. Revere signaled Brown Beauty to slow down again. Filigree was puzzled.

"Are we at Lexington already?" he asked Brown Beauty.

"You don't know anything, do you?" the horse answered.

Mr. Revere turned onto a narrow dirt path that led to a small farmhouse. He leaped off Brown Beauty and knocked on the door.

A woman opened it. Mr. Revere said quietly, "The Regulars are coming out. Have you got someone to ride to Sudbury to alert their militia? We need all of our Minutemen to get to Concord."

The woman nodded. "Our boy Jed's ready and waiting."

Now Filigree understood. "He's trying to get more people to ride to Concord!" he said to Brown Beauty.

"Glad you're catching up," Brown Beauty snorted.

"Quiet, now," the woman whispered to Mr. Revere. "The Fenwicks across the road are loyal to the crown. Too many families around here are loyalists."

As Mr. Revere walked back to Brown Beauty, Filigree saw him glance uneasily across the road.

"I have an idea," he said to Filigree. "Do exactly what I say."

From then on, when they stopped at a house, Mr. Revere didn't knock. Instead he lifted Filigree from his bag and whispered, "Speak." Filigree barked softly until someone in the house woke up and came to the door. Then Mr. Revere leaned in to whisper to them, "The Regulars are coming out," and slipped quietly away.

One farmer leaned over to scratch

Filigree's ears. "That's clever," he muttered. "Loyalists might wonder what was up if they heard a knock on their neighbor's door in the middle of the night. No one is going to think about a quiet bark or two."

"Don't get too full of yourself," Brown Beauty grumbled to Filigree as they galloped away.

They rode on, warning patriots along the way. Finally they crossed Lexington Common in the darkness.

"We did it, boy," Mr. Revere said low.

Filigree felt warm all over. His fur was no longer damp, but it wasn't that. It was a glow that started deep inside him. Now he knew, for certain, that he was helping Mr. Revere and the patriots. "There it is," Mr. Revere murmured. "Reverend Clarke's house. Time to wake up Adams and Hancock."

He spurred Brown Beauty forward.

11
Mr. Adams and Mr. Hancock

Mr. Revere burst through Reverend Clarke's doorway. Filigree jumped from his bag onto the floor. Mr. Revere went into the large parlor. Filigree scrambled after him. There on the hearth lay Jove.

The big Newfoundland lifted his head.

He looked like he had never been so sur-prised to see another dog in his life.

Filigree lowered his ears and wagged his tail. He didn't want Jove to stand on him again. Mr. Adams and Mr. Hancock stumbled into the room in their nightshirts. Reverend Clarke came down the stairs.

"Adams. Hancock," Mr. Revere said, taking off his spurs and coat. "Gage's men know where you are and they're coming for you. You've got to head out *now*."

Filigree felt something

big looming over him. He looked to see Jove staring down at him. Jove's breath was warm on his face. He sniffed at Filigree.

"What are you doing here?" Jove woofed. It was like he couldn't believe his nose.

Filigree wanted to sound like things like this happened all the time. But he couldn't. He woofed back proudly, "I've been helping Mr. Revere."

"You, Dormouse?" Jove laughed. "*You?*"

"I see you brought your daughter's little dog, Revere," said Mr. Adams.

Filigree wished Mr. Adams hadn't called him "little" right in front of Jove.

"Yes," Mr. Revere said. "He helped me warn all the families on the way. And he sniffed out every Redcoat patrol between here and Charlestown Common. I'd never have gotten here safely without him."

Jove grunted. "I see. Assembling the troops."

Jove looked at the hearth. On the stone were some cornbread and sausages. Jove always told the pack how Mr. Adams saved him the nicest scraps. He looked back at Filigree. "I was just about to tuck in," he said. "Join me?"

Stunned, Filigree yipped a "yes."

He scampered to the hearth and gulped down a sausage before Jove could change his mind. Then he started on the cornbread. Jove ate the rest and told him what was going on.

"My master spent half the night convincing Hancock he can't fight with the militia himself," he said.

"Why can't he?" Filigree asked.

Jove puffed out his chest. "He and my master are too important! The patriots need them. But try telling that fool Hancock that."

Mr. Revere's voice startled them both. It cut through the warmth of the room like a knife.

"Where's Dawes?" he demanded. "He was on a slow horse, but he left before I did. He should be here by now. Reverend Clarke? Any sign of him?"

"Nothing," said Reverend Clarke.

Filigree saw Mr. Revere's jaw tighten.

"Redcoats chased us on the way here," Filigree told Jove.

"They might have caught Dawes," rumbled Jove. "Maybe even all the other riders. That's a worry."

"I hope not," Filigree said. He liked Mr. Dawes. But at least Mr. Revere, with Filigree's help, had completed his mission.

Mr. Adams and Mr. Hancock knew they had to escape.

"What happens now?" Filigree asked Jove.

Before Jove could answer, the room was suddenly full of bustle. Other people came downstairs. One of them was Mrs. Clarke, the reverend's wife. Another woman came from the kitchen with platters of food.

"You'll need some nourishment," she said. Jove told Filigree she was Miss Quincy and was going to marry Mr. Hancock. Some other men knocked on the door—Filigree hoped one of them was Mr. Dawes, but they were from the village. They spoke urgently to Mr.

Revere and Reverend Clarke. Filigree heard something about the militia. Mr. Adams and Mr. Hancock went into the next room and came back dressed. But then they started running back and forth between the rooms, looking for things.

"Mr. Revere said they had to leave *now*!" Filigree barked at Jove.

"That's just how people talk," Jove said. "But they never just go. They always seem to have to find things and pack things and do things first. Not like us dogs."

Mr. Revere paced. Filigree was so tense, he almost jumped out of his fur when the door flew open and a man strode in.

"It's Mr. Dawes!" Filigree said. "He made it!"

"Glad he's in one piece," Jove said.

Mr. Dawes was disguised as a farmer to fool the Redcoats. He was breathing hard.

"The country is alive with British patrols," he said. "I don't know if anyone at all made it to Concord."

Mr. Revere didn't say anything. He just walked over to a chair, sat in it, and started to put on his spurs. Dawes nodded at him. He didn't even sit down.

"You've been riding all night, Revere," Clarke said. "It's after midnight. You're exhausted. You too, Dawes. We'll find someone else."

"We have to make sure at least one rider gets through to Concord," Mr. Revere answered. He stood up. "And you know very well there are no better riders than Dawes and me."

"He's just being nice about Mr. Dawes," Filigree told Jove proudly. "Everyone knows Mr. Revere is the fastest rider in Massachusetts."

John Hancock picked up his sword. "I'll go!" he boomed. "I'll fight any Regular who gets in my way."

"That fool," Jove muttered.

Mr. Adams took the sword from Mr. Hancock. "Now, John," he said. "We've talked about this."

"I'll get the horses," said Mr. Dawes. "Adams, Hancock—you head to Watertown, away from the Regulars. Revere, I'll meet you outside."

Mr. Revere walked to the door. Filigree started to follow and then stopped. Mr. Revere had been so angry with him for following before.

Jove shoved him with his nose. "What are you waiting for?" he barked.

Mr. Revere turned back.

"Coming, boy?" he said. "Can't do it without you."

Filigree's heart soared like an eagle. He had never felt this way before. He ran to Mr. Revere. Together they set out into the night.

12
Capture

"I see them, boy," Mr. Revere breathed. Two Redcoat officers sat on their horses at a narrow bend in the road. Filigree didn't dare bark or even whimper. He had warned Mr. Revere by nudging him on the chest with his nose.

After they'd left Reverend Clarke's house,

they'd run into another rider, Mr. Prescott.
He was a Son of Liberty and had offered to
help. So now there were three of them trying
to get to Concord.

Mr. Prescott and Mr. Dawes were behind
them. Mr. Revere called quietly, "Dawes!
Prescott! Regulars straight ahead! There are
only two of them. We can get through."

But something was wrong. Filigree knew
it. There weren't just two Redcoat scents.

They were everywhere.

Frantically he pushed his head against
Mr. Revere. He even barked. It was too late.

Two other Redcoats emerged from the

woods. All four rode toward Mr. Revere. Their swords were in their hands. Their pistols were at their sides.

"Stop!" one of them shouted. "If you go an inch further, you are a dead man!"

Right then, Mr. Prescott and Mr. Dawes rode up. The three patriots spurred their horses forward. They were going to try to ride through all the soldiers! Brown Beauty called a challenge and galloped. *Faster, faster!* Filigree pleaded silently.

But the soldiers rode straight toward the patriots. They drew their pistols.

"Into that pasture or we'll shoot!" they called. Filigree heard the sharp clicks of them cocking their guns. The patriots stopped. They were surrounded.

One of the soldiers pointed to a pasture at the side of the road. The Redcoats herded the three patriot riders toward it.

Why couldn't I find a way to tell him there

were so many? Filigree said to himself. *I should have found a way.*

Brown Beauty whinnied angrily. Mr. Revere shushed her. But Filigree had understood her even if Mr. Revere couldn't. "Can you get away, dog?" she'd asked. "Go for help?"

How? thought Filigree, though he didn't dare even snuffle.

Suddenly he heard Mr. Prescott's voice. "PUT ON!" Mr. Prescott cried at the top of his lungs. Brown Beauty took off at full speed. Filigree heard Mr. Prescott's horse galloping to the left. Brown Beauty was headed for the woods beyond the pasture. Mr. Revere was half standing in his saddle.

"What's he doing?" Filigree cried under the sound of Brown Beauty's gallop.

"It's a trick we've used before," Brown Beauty answered. "If he jumps off when we're hidden by the trees, the soldiers might not see him. They'll follow me instead. And then they'd better watch out."

Filigree braced himself to land hard.

Brown Beauty's hooves pounded. Filigree lost track of Mr. Prescott and Mr. Dawes. Brown Beauty came closer and closer to the trees. It looked like she was going to run into a tall pine. He told himself that neither Mr. Revere nor Brown Beauty would let that happen. The smells of Redcoats and horses were all around them. He couldn't tell one scent from another. But they were almost to the safety of the woods. They were going to make it!

Something moved at the corner of Filigree's eye. Six more Redcoats on horse-back emerged from the trees, three on each side of Brown Beauty.

Three of them grabbed her bridle. She reared up, but the men hung on. Filigree ducked down so the flap of the bag hid his head, but he could still see out. Brown Beauty landed back on all four hooves.

A second later, six Redcoat pistols were pressed against Mr. Revere's chest.

13
Escape!

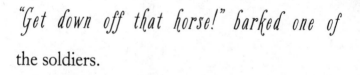

"Get down off that horse!" barked one of the soldiers.

Mr. Revere did.

Redcoats surrounded him. Filigree didn't see Mr. Dawes or Mr. Prescott anywhere. He saw several other prisoners, though. The Redcoats had been busy.

One of the soldiers spoke. Filigree thought he must be the officer in charge.

"Where have you come from, sir?" he asked. Filigree was surprised at how polite he was.

"Why, Boston," Mr. Revere answered, just as politely.

The officer paused. "Sir, may I crave your name?"

"Revere."

"What?" said the officer. "*Paul* Revere?"

"Yes."

"The Yankee spy?" one of the men grunted.

Filigree was frantic. *Why was Mr. Revere telling them who he was?*

Some of the soldiers began to shout
insults. One of them shoved Mr. Revere
hard. Another grabbed him from behind by
both arms. A third put his face right up into

Mr. Revere's. "Rebel villain!" he shouted.

Filigree forced himself not to growl. He couldn't help Mr. Revere if he was seen or heard. He ducked down all the way into the bag.

The officer in charge spoke. "Enough!" he thundered. "We are not ruffians, we are British officers! And we will behave with honor and courtesy! Take your hands from that man."

Filigree couldn't see what was going on, but he felt Mr. Revere shrug off the soldiers. He heard Brown Beauty scrape her hoof in the dirt. He realized the Redcoats must still be holding her. He could imagine how she was glaring at them.

The officer in charge said, "Don't be afraid, sir. I'll guarantee your safety as long as you behave with honor yourself."

"If I were you," said Mr. Revere, "I wouldn't waste time worrying about me. You've treated me decently, sir. I'll do the same and give you a warning. Your plans are known. There will be five hundred patriots in Lexington soon. They might already be there waiting for you. And your fellow soldiers are not coming to help you. Your boats all ran aground. They're stuck in the mud in the Charles River."

No, they're not, thought Filigree. *Mr. Revere is tricking them.*

Mr. Revere kept talking. "If you value your lives, you'll get away from Lexington and Concord and go back to Boston as quick as you can."

Filigree heard the stunned silence that followed this. One of the officers said, "That's impossible. We have fifteen hundred men on the way." The tension in his voice told Filigree he wasn't so sure.

"Do we?" said another. He sounded nervous.

"I'll find out," said the officer in charge.

"Come with me, Captain." Filigree heard horses galloping away.

"I've got to get them to think the militia is already in Lexington," Mr. Revere said under his breath. No one but Filigree could have heard him. "I've got to keep them away from there."

Now Filigree understood why Mr. Revere had told the officers the truth about who he was. It was to gain their trust. Now they would believe the other things he said. He couldn't fight them all, so he was trying to outsmart them.

A snarling British voice made Filigree

flinch. "I'm going to ask you some questions," it said. "And I'm not as pleasant as our commanding officer. If you don't tell *me* the truth, I'll blow your brains out."

Filigree heard the sound of a pistol being cocked. Brown Beauty neighed angrily. Filigree choked on his breath.

Mr. Revere sounded as calm as if he were discussing a silver teapot with a customer in his shop. "I don't know what right you think you have to stop me on the road and make me your prisoner," he said. "But I'm a truthful man, and I'll tell you the truth. I'm not afraid."

I am, thought Filigree.

The soldier asked the same questions the other man had. Mr. Revere gave the same answers. When he said again that there were five hundred militia men waiting in Lexington, the soldier lost his temper.

"Why would Paul Revere, the rebel spy, want us to stay away from Lexington?" he shouted. "To save our lives? I don't think so. I don't believe you *do* have any armed men there. What's in Lexington that you don't want us to see, Revere? We're going there, and you're coming with us. Search him for pistols, men!"

The other officers patted Mr. Revere all over. Filigree curled himself up as small as he could in the corner of the bag.

It did no good. A soldier grabbed it and felt something inside. He opened it. He burst out laughing. He tore the bag off Mr. Revere and shook it out. Filigree fell to the ground.

"Look at this!" the soldier cried. "The great spy Paul Revere's got a little lapdog with him!"

Filigree scrambled to his feet. He was surrounded by a circle of Redcoats. "I am NOT a lapdog!" he growled at them. "I'm a patriot!"

"Shh, boy. Careful," Mr. Revere whispered between his teeth.

All the soldiers were laughing at Filigree now. The Redcoats thought he was a joke. They'd never met a patriot dog before. And this time, Filigree knew it wouldn't help to fight them. He had a better idea.

"Distract the Redcoats," he woofed to Brown Beauty. "Um, please?"

"Gladly," Brown Beauty said. She lowered her head and kicked up her back legs. Then she reared up and screamed in fury. The British shouted and grabbed at her.

Filigree darted between one of the officers' legs. The officer reached down to grab

him, but Filigree was too quick. He slipped through his hands.

"Here, catch him!" called the man.

"It's just a silly little dog," said the mean officer. "Grab that mare!"

"Calm down, girl," Filigree heard Mr. Revere say to Brown Beauty. Filigree didn't know if either of them had seen him escape.

"Get on your horse, Revere," an officer said. "We're going to Lexington. If you try to get away, we'll shoot you. Grab his reins, one of you."

Filigree didn't hear anything else. He

was already rushing into the woods.

If Mr. Revere couldn't keep the men away from Mr. Hancock and Mr. Adams in Lexington, maybe he could.

But he had no idea how.

14
The Plan

Filigree flung himself down next to the belfry at the edge of Lexington Common. He'd never run so far and fast in his life. He'd done it in short bursts. All he cared about was staying ahead of the Redcoat patrol. If he hadn't jumped on a wagon full of wood heading past the town, he would never have

 made it in time.

He was covered in mud from his paws to his ears. Even his nose was full of mud. He'd had to cross the swamp by the graveyard to stay out of sight.

The houses of the town were dark, but light from Buckman Tavern spilled out across the road. Now that Filigree was here,

he wasn't sure what to do. If he went back to Reverend Clarke's house without Mr. Revere, they would guess that something was wrong. But there was no way for him to tell them about having to keep the patrol away. And the house was past the far end of town. By the time Filigree got there, it might be too late.

Something huge and dog-shaped crossed in front of Buckman Tavern. Relief washed over Filigree. Only one dog could be that big. Jove would know what to do!

Filigree ran toward him. And straight into a man hiding beside the little shed that stood between the belfry and the tavern. Filigree's nose was so full of mud, he hadn't smelled a thing.

In the moonlight, Filigree saw that the man was tall with a pale face. It was the Redcoat from the fight that afternoon on Back Street! The same one who had tried to smash Jove's head in! But he wasn't wearing a uniform. He was in ordinary clothes. He stared at Filigree.

"YOU. LITTLE. *RAT!*" he whispered.

There weren't supposed to be any British soldiers in Lexington yet.

"Everyone laughed at me," the Redcoat

growled. "Said I couldn't even fight a yippy little dog. The captain said I was useless and sent me here to wait in the dark."

He's a spy! Filigree realized.

Another man stepped out from behind the shed. It was the shorter Redcoat from that afternoon. He wore ordinary clothes too.

The tall soldier swung his musket off his shoulder. "I'll teach you to get in the way of one of King George's best fighters!" he snarled at Filigree. He reached into a pouch at his waist and pulled out a paper wad stuffed with what smelled like gunpowder. Within seconds, he'd cocked the gun, bit off the top of the paper wad, and poured some powder into the firing pan. Then he stuffed the rest of the wad into the barrel of the mus- ket. His gun was loaded!

Filigree bolted across the road to the tav- ern. He swerved sharply back and forth.

The Redcoat fired. The dirt just to the

left of Filigree exploded. He yipped and kept on running.

"You fool!" he heard the shorter Redcoat whisper. "We're supposed to be quiet! That shot could be heard all the way to Charlestown! If you fire again, I swear I'll tell General Gage himself. Understand? I'm going to see what's happening across the Common. You stay here and be quiet." Filigree heard him stomp away.

Filigree reached Jove. His ears hurt from the sound of the shot, and he was panting so hard, his ribs ached. "There are Redcoats hiding on the Common!" he yipped breathlessly.

"There are what? Who fired that shot?"

"The REDCOAT!" Filigree woofed, shaking. "Why isn't anyone coming out of the tavern to find him? He *shot* at me!"

"People shoot off muskets all the time," Jove rumbled. "They have to empty their guns just to come into the tavern so they don't fire them by mistake. And I don't see what you're so upset about. He missed."

He didn't miss by much! Filigree wanted to say. But Jove was watching him. Filigree made himself stop shaking. Jove woofed in approval.

"Now," the big dog said, "what are you doing here? Where's your master?"

Filigree told Jove that Mr. Revere had been captured, and that a Redcoat patrol was on its way.

"We have to stop them before they get here," Filigree panted. "They'll find *your* master! Why are you still here?"

"They're still at Reverend Clarke's house trying to pack all our secret papers into a trunk," Jove answered. "Where's that patrol? Sounds like Mr. Revere could use my help. Those Redcoats won't know what hit them when I'm through." He started toward the road.

Filigree jumped in front of him. Jove

stopped, startled. Filigree was startled too. A few hours ago, he would never have stood between Jove and where he wanted to go.

"We can't stop them that way," he told the big Newfoundland. "There are too many of them. We have to trick them. Mr. Revere did that." *Frances did too, on the wharf,* Filigree remembered. "When you fight a bigger enemy, you have to be smarter than they are."

"How?" Jove asked. Filigree realized that Jove had probably never fought a bigger enemy.

"We have to make them think that there

are armed patriots waiting for them here," Filigree told him. "That's what Mr. Revere told the patrol."

"Well, then, what's your plan, Dormouse?" Jove asked. Filigree gulped. He never thought that Jove would ask him anything.

They were running out of time. The patrol would be in Lexington any minute. And that Redcoat spy was watching the patriots' every move.

Then he remembered what the shorter Redcoat had said: *That shot could be heard all the way to Charlestown.*

And then Filigree knew what he had to do.

If it worked, he could save Mr. Revere and stop the patrol from coming to Lexington. Mr. Adams and Mr. Hancock would be safe. If it didn't . . .

"Jove," Filigree said, "I need your help."

15
The Battle

"Can you get the militia men out of the tavern?" Filigree asked Jove. "The more the better."

"I'd rather fight some Redcoats," Jove grumbled. But he pushed open the heavy door of the tavern. It stuck open. He shuffled inside. The sound of men talking in urgent whispers drifted out.

Filigree took off at a run.

The tall Redcoat was still beside the shed. Filigree barked to get his attention.

Blood rushed to the soldier's face.

"Are you mocking me, rat?" he said. He stepped toward Filigree. Filigree took a step backward. He barked again.

The soldier ran at him. Filigree darted in a circle around him.

The soldier picked up a big stick. He swung it. Filigree ducked and the soldier fell onto his hands and knees.

He grabbed for Filigree. Filigree dashed across the road. The soldier got up and followed. Filigree's fur was standing straight up. But he had to get the soldier closer to Buckman Tavern.

Suddenly the soldier stopped. The men inside the tavern were shouting and laughing. The Redcoat realized how close he was to them and started to move away.

"Not so fast, Lobsterback!" Filigree barked. He grabbed the leg of the soldier's pants and pulled. He tore a piece of cloth from it and fell onto his rump.

The soldier hissed in anger and tried to stomp Filigree. Filigree barely scrambled out of the way.

Hurry up, Jove, he thought.

There was a stable across from the tavern. Filigree could smell the horses inside. He backed against the stable wall. The soldier followed. Filigree was cornered. The soldier grinned down at him.

"There's about to be one less cur in Lexington," he said. "And I don't even need to shoot you." He lifted his boot up high. Filigree tried to woof, but his breath was stuck in his chest. His legs screamed at him to run, but he had to wait. The plan would fail if the Redcoat spy left too soon.

He heard a crash and a shout. Jove burst out of the tavern. He was carrying two muskets in his jaws.

The soldier's boot came down fast. At the very last instant, Filigree dodged. The Redcoat stumbled.

At least six patriots ran out of the tavern after Jove, still laughing and shouting. They all had their muskets and pistols. The Redcoat saw them and bolted for the trees.

"Look there!" a patriot shouted.

Quickly the men loaded their muskets. Then they all aimed and fired. *BANG, BANG, BANG, BANG, BANG, BANG!*

The loud gunfire made Filigree yelp.

His legs gave way under him. He couldn't believe it. His plan had worked! The men had fired at the Redcoat spy! Now he could only hope that it was enough.

An older man came out of the tavern. "Quiet!" he said to the militia men.

"We saw someone in the dark," one of the men said. "A spy, maybe."

"Or a possum," the older man muttered. "The Redcoats aren't here yet. And what in tarnation are you doing making so much noise? Get inside and stop imagining things."

The men grumbled. But they filed back inside.

Jove walked up to Filigree, chuckling.

Filigree looked up at him. "You stole their guns???"

"You didn't say *how* you wanted 'em out of the tavern," Jove grunted. He sauntered across the road. Together they stood guard at the edge of Lexington Common. Moments later, Filigree heard hoof beats. It was the Redcoat patrol! They stopped almost right next to Filigree and Jove.

Filigree's heart sank. The patrol had come to Lexington anyway. They would search the town! They would find Mr. Adams and Mr. Hancock, and the militia, too!

But the soldiers didn't ride any farther

into town. Instead, they talked in whispers. They seemed to come to a decision. Then they spurred their horses and rode on away from Lexington.

"Well done, patriot," Jove said.

Filigree was too surprised to even wag his tail.

Filigree and Jove waited at the edge of town. At last they heard familiar footsteps. Three shapes moved carefully through the swamp. Filigree recognized the one in the lead immediately. Mr. Revere crept through the darkness.

Filigree raced toward him. Jove followed at a quick march.

"Filigree!" Mr. Revere grinned. "Good boy. And if it isn't Jove!" He patted Filigree's head. "You'll never guess what happened. The Redcoats brought me almost here. Then they heard a volley of musket fire. It made them believe my story that we had hundreds of militia in Lexington! They said they were

going to ride straight past town. They let us all go and got out of there."

He stopped and looked down at Filigree. "Now, you wouldn't know anything about that, would you, boy?"

Filigree yipped joyfully. The patriot leaders were safe, and the militia was gathering.

He could feel that the night was far from over, and that the real fight was still to come. The patriots—including Filigree—would be ready for it.

Epilogue

July 1775, Watertown, Massachusetts

"Filigree!" Frances called out from the edge of Watertown Common. "Race you to that oak tree! And you, Jove!" Mr. Adams was in Watertown too.

She had almost won when Mr. Revere appeared across the common. Frances, Jove, and Filigree all fell over one another in a heap of arms, legs, and paws. Frances giggled and even Jove laughed.

"There's my girl!" Mr. Revere said to Frances as he reached them. He patted Filigree's head. "Strong as . . . as . . ."

"Filigree?" laughed Frances. Anvil lay

curled in the sunshine just out of the shade of the oak tree. She lifted her head, blinked at Filigree, and went back to sleep.

"One more time?" Frances said to the dogs.

Just a few hours after Mr. Revere had made it safely to town, the Battle of Lexington had begun. The patriots had been ready, thanks to the midnight riders. But it meant that the patriot fighters couldn't go back to Boston.

Mr. Revere had his family meet him in Watertown as soon as he could. Ever since her nighttime adventure on the streets of Boston, Frances just wouldn't stay in bed and inside any longer. Little by little, Mr. Revere realized she was strong now. He hadn't treated her like a weakling since she arrived in Watertown.

Mr. Revere hadn't told anyone about Filigree's help that night. That was their secret. "I might need you again, boy," Mr. Revere had said to him. "A spy never reveals his best weapons." And of course, he never knew exactly how Filigree had helped him escape the Redcoats and scare them away from Lexington.

But Jove did, and word had spread. Now every dog in the Massachusetts Bay Colony knew how Filigree had helped the patriot cause.

Frances took off running across the common.

"Think you can keep up, Dormouse?" Jove said.

This time, Filigree didn't mind the nickname.

Authors' Note

The Midnight Ride
of Paul Revere

M any people have heard or read Henry
Wadsworth Longfellow's famous poem
"Paul Revere's Ride," which was published
in 1861. It's an exciting poem, but the real
story is pretty different. We based our story
on a report called a *deposition* that Paul Revere

wrote in 1775, telling his story of the ride. We also read a lot of books and accounts of the midnight ride, and talked to people who work at the Paul Revere House in Boston and the Lexington Historical Society.

Paul Revere never did shout, "The British are coming!" He would have needed to warn the patriots very quietly, because the countryside was full of British patrols. Also, many people in the colonies were still loyal to England's King George, and Revere would not have wanted *them* to know what the patriots were up to. Paul Revere was also not a lone hero. Other patriot riders were out that night, spreading the word, including William Dawes.

Many people think that Revere's main mission was to ride to Concord and alert the patriots that the British patrols were coming. Instead, his job was to get to Lexington, which is halfway between Boston and Concord, to warn John Hancock and Samuel Adams they were about to be arrested. He went on to Concord afterward because the patriots didn't know if anyone had made it there. No one knows exactly what Adams and Hancock were doing after Revere left or why they took so long to leave town. Sources say they even went to the tavern to get "refreshment"!

Paul Revere really was captured by a British patrol on the way to Concord. And gunshots fired from Lexington really did convince the British patrol to let their prisoners go and to ride away from the town. No one knows who fired the shots, and there is nothing to say that a little dog did not make it happen.

Paul Revere had many children, including a daughter named Frances, who was nine years old at the time of the ride. Very little is known about her, and we added her illness to the story. No one knows if Paul Revere had either a Pomeranian or a house cat. However, Samuel Adams's big Newfoundland, who was trained to bark and nip at Redcoats, was real. His name was probably Queue, but for our story, we named him Jove. There were laws against keeping big dogs in Boston. Samuel Adams doesn't seem to have paid any attention to them at all.

General Thomas Gage was the leader of the British troops in Boston. Some of his troops thought he was too nice and gentlemanly to the patriots. His American wife, Margaret, may have been a spy for the patriots. He eventually sent her away to England. Mrs. Banks and Mr. Banks weren't real people, but we added them to represent the loyalists in Boston.

Paul Revere's friend Robert Newman was one of three people who took the job of lighting the lanterns in the Old North Church. The others were John Pulling and Thomas Bernard. Two of Revere's friends, Joshua Bentley and Thomas Richardson, rowed him across the Charles River. The nearly full moon really was unusually low in the sky that night, which very likely helped Revere get across the river without being seen. John Larkin's speedy mare, Brown Beauty, was real too.

A few hours after Paul Revere made it safely back to Lexington, another shot was fired on Lexington Common. Revere heard it, but he was busy helping John Hancock move a trunk full of important papers. This shot is often called "the shot heard round the world." It started the Battles of Lexington and Concord, and was the beginning of the American Revolution.

Some Information About Slavery in Massachusetts

*I*t is important to remember that there were slaves in Boston and throughout the Massachusetts Bay Colony. The first record of slavery in Boston dates from 1638. It was abolished in Massachusetts in 1783. There is no data or documentation that shows that the

Revere family owned slaves.

However, many people in the colony, patriot and loyalist alike, owned slaves and profited from slavery. Even after slavery was abolished in Massachusetts, many people continued to be subjected to discrimination and slavery conditions.

We also know that slaves took part in spreading the word that the British were on their way on the night of the midnight ride. In the town of Needham, for example, a slave named Abel Benson warned some of the town with blasts on his trumpet after an unknown patriot rider stopped there.

Along with people of African descent who were slaves, there were also those who were free who lived in Boston and the Massachusetts area. Some individuals born in the colonies were part African and part another nationality. For example, Crispus Attucks was of both African and Native American decent. He worked as a stevedore (someone who loads and unloads ships). He died in the Boston Massacre. Even free people of African descent lived under some threat of being cast into slavery.

Both slaves and free men of African or multiracial descent fought in the American

Revolution. Prince Estabrook was an African slave who was wounded in the Battle of Lexington Common and received his freedom by fighting in the Revolution. Some slaves who fought were freed. However, many were not.

Acknowledgments

When we got the idea for the At the Heels of History series, we could only have dreamed of working with a team as skilled and supportive as the one at Margaret K. McElderry Books. Heartfelt thanks to the wonderful Ruta Rimas and Nicole Fiorica, whose editorial guidance and advice strengthened and enriched this book, and to illustrator Claire Powell, whose talents brought Filigree's adventures to life.

A million thanks to the always brilliant Mollie Glick and the team at CAA, with a special shout-out to Emily Westcott, whose early feedback helped us imagine the dogs of Filigree's world.

Many thanks to Patrick Leehey and Alex Powell at the Paul Revere House for sharing their research and knowledge, and to Chris Kauffman and Sarah McDonough at the Lexington Historical Society. Thank you to Dr. Carla Walter for her insights and guidance on the experience of people of African descent in colonial Massachusetts, and to Nick Grossman and Ruel Mac for detailed information on eighteenth-century guns. Thanks to Dian Bodiford for cat consultation. David Hackett Fischer's *Paul Revere's Ride* was an invaluable resource. Thank you to the Berkeley Public Library and Contra Costa Public Library for the wealth of information within their walls.

We could not have written this book without the guidance and support of our writing partners:

Lucy Jane Bledsoe,
Michelle Hackel,
Mary Mackey, Lisa
Riddiough, and Elizabeth Stark. Thank you
to Debbie Notkin for helping us successfully
navigate the world of coauthoring a creative
project.

Pam would like to thank Max and
Caspian for their patience and understanding
while Mom was busy writing, and her husband, Mehran, and sister, Brenna, for their
support and love. Dorothy would like to
thank her family and friends for their love,
encouragement, and support. None of this

happens without all of you. Thank you to the San Francisco Writers' Grotto and Word of Mouth Bay Area. And, of course, thank you to dogs. You're all very good dogs.